Hugh Lewin
and Lisa Kopper

A Well in the Desert

Hamish Hamilton · London

182041

To Abdoul, Thierno,
and their friends in Senegal,
for their work in making the desert green

HAMISH HAMILTON CHILDREN'S BOOKS

Published by the Penguin Group
27 Wrights Lane, London W8 5TZ, England
Viking Penguin Inc, 40 West 23rd Street, New York, New York 10010, U.S.A.
Penguin Books Australia Ltd, Ringwood, Victoria, Australia
Penguin Books Canada Ltd, 2801 John Street, Markham, Ontario, Canada L3R 1B4
Penguin Books (N.Z.) Ltd, 182–190 Wairau Road, Auckland 10, New Zealand

Penguin Books Ltd, Registered Offices: Harmondsworth, Middlesex, England

First published in Great Britain 1989 by
Hamish Hamilton Children's Books

Text Copyright © 1989 by Hugh Lewin
Illustrations Copyright © 1989 by Lisa Kopper

1 3 5 7 9 10 8 6 4 2

British Library Cataloguing in Publication Data
A CIP catalogue record for this book
is available from the British Library

ISBN 0-241-12213-9
Printed in Hong Kong

Mahmadou the fisherman is the most important man in the village. He can talk to crocodiles and walk with lions.

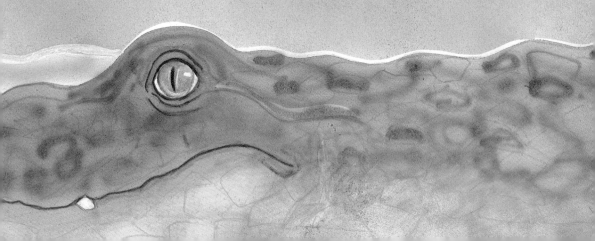

He does that when the rains come and the river floods. Then foreign crocodiles and lions come into our valley and kill the cattle.

But it hasn't rained for a long time and he is not happy.
He sits by the fire, running sand through his fingers and
muttering.

Twice we've planted the crops and tried to water them. But the river is far away and there's little water left.

The crops have shrivelled and there's no grain
in the store. We are very hungry and Mahmadou
mutters long into the night.

The elders have called a meeting and decided to dig a deep hole in the sand, looking for the underground river.

Mahmadou doesn't think we'll find water. He says he's never seen a crocodile under the ground. So he sits all day under the tree, glaring at us and watching the sky.

But now the well is dug and ready. It's very deep, so we have to use donkeys to help us pull up the water.

We start at the well when the sun rises. The donkeys pull all day, while we run with the water bags to feed the new crop patch.

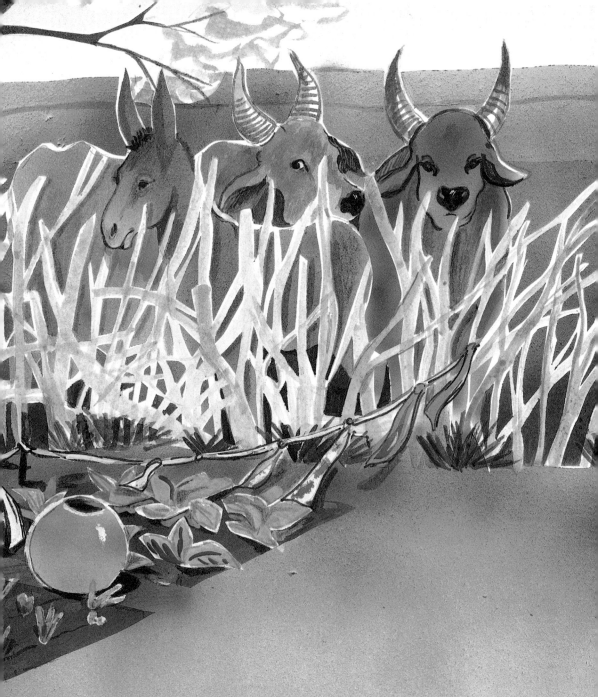

We've planted rows of vegetables and built a strong
hedge around the garden to keep the animals out.

We gave the first ripe tomato to Mahmadou.
He looked at it for a long time before
chewing it, very slowly.

Then he went to the well and peered down, long and hard. He walked away, shaking his head.

We found him by the river, preparing his fishing lines.
It's going to rain again soon, he says, and then the
crocodiles will return with the flood. And the lions.